From the Books of
HEATHER HORNUNG

D1179832

Tales of the Rue Broca

NOS
GLACES

Tales of the Rue Broca

BY PIERRE GRIPARI

Translated by Doriane Grutman

Illustrated by Emily McCully

THE BOBBS-MERRILL COMPANY, INC.

Indianapolis New York

The Bobbs-Merrill Company, Inc.
A Subsidiary of Howard W. Sams & Co., Inc.
Publishers Indianapolis Kansas City New York

Copyright © 1967 by Editions de la Table Ronde
English translation copyright © 1969 by Bobbs-Merrill
Illustrations copyright © 1969 by Emily McCully
Printed in the United States of America
All rights reserved
Library of Congress Catalog Card Number: 70–78282
First English language edition
Selections from CONTES DE LA RUE BROCA published in France in 1967

Contents

Preface

It is a well-known fact that children understand everything. If I could be sure that they alone were going to read this book, it would not occur to me to write a preface. But as these tales will no doubt fall into the hands of grown-ups as well, I believe I should offer some explanation.

Broca Street is unlike any other street in Paris. If you take a map, you will see—or think you see—that Broca Street crosses Port-Royal Boulevard. If, accepting this evidence, you get into your car and ride down Port-Royal Boulevard expecting to come to Broca Street, you will find yourself driving up and down endlessly without ever finding it.

You will not find the reason for this phenomenon on

the map, because the map has only two dimensions. The fact is that, like Einstein's universe, Paris in this particular spot is a curve and passes over itself, as it were. I must apologize for using the jargon of science fiction, but there is really no other way to put it. Broca Street is a depression, a groove, a descent in a sub-space of three dimensions.

The best thing is to leave your car at the garage and go by foot down Port-Royal Boulevard. As you walk along, the buildings on your right will at one point disappear, and soon, ahead of you, you will see a stairway which sinks down into the bowels of the earth. Do not be afraid to descend. Once at the bottom, you will see that though you are below ground, you are still above ground, in the open air, but in another level of Paris. Above you, there will be something which looks like a bridge, but which is in fact Port-Royal Boulevard, which you have just left.

This may seem strange, but that's how it is.

In any event, as you look around, you will see that you are on a narrow, winding street lined with shops and houses. You are on Broca Street!

This little street all by itself constitutes a small village and has its own special atmosphere. In the first place, the people all know each other, and each of them pretty well knows what the others are up to and how they spend their time, which is exceptional in a city like Paris.

In the second place, they are, for the most part, of very diverse backgrounds, and only rarely Parisian. In this street I have met Algerians, Spaniards, Portuguese, Italians, a Pole, a Russian . . . even some Frenchmen!

Finally, the people of Broca Street have yet another thing in common: they love stories.

I have had plenty of bad luck in my literary career, which I attribute mostly to the fact that the French in general—and Parisians in particular—do not like fiction. They crave facts, or the appearance of facts—realism. As for me, the only stories that truly interest me are those that never have taken place, never can and never will take place. An imaginary story does not have to justify its existence with documentary evidence. Therefore it has a greater chance of containing profound truths than stories that are based on life. In this regard I am—perhaps I say this to console myself—more realistic in my own way than all those people who, believing they love truth, allow their lives to be governed by stupid lies which are stupid enough to sound like the truth!

And now, after I have taken such a strong position in favor of fiction, I myself will tell you a true story. Here it is:

At No. 69 Broca Street there is a general store, the owner of which, Papa Saïd, is an Algerian married to a Breton. At the time of which I speak, there were four children: three girls and a boy (a fifth has since been added). The eldest daughter is called Nadia, the second Malika, and the third Rachida, and the little boy is called Bachir.

In a hotel next to the general store lives, among

others, a certain Monsieur Riccardi, who, as his name indicates, is an Italian, and who is also the father of four children. The eldest is called Nicholas and the youngest Tina. I will not mention other names. That would be pointless and only make for confusion.

Nicholas Riccardi, the Saïd children, and all the children of Broca Street often played together. One fine day an odd character by the name of Monsieur Pierre suddenly appeared. He was tall, with brown crew-cut hair, brown and green eyes, and eyeglasses. He always needed a shave and every day he sported what looked like a two-days' growth of beard. (In fact, people wondered how he managed to permanently keep it at a two-days' growth.) Whatever he wore looked as though it were about to fall apart. He was forty years old, a bachelor, and lived above, on Port-Royal Boulevard.

His tastes were simple: he seemed to exist mainly on crackers and chocolate; he had fruit when it was available, and he would wash it all down with endless cups of light coffee or mint tea.

When asked about his occupation, he would reply that he was a writer. As his books were nowhere to be seen, especially not in bookshops, this reply convinced no one. And the residents of Broca Street wondered for a long time how he was able to earn a living.

When I speak of the residents, I refer only to the grown-ups. For the children knew from the start that Monsieur Pierre was not a man at all but an old witch in disguise. They also knew that a witch must be unmasked and forced to reveal her real self. So they would dance around Monsieur Pierre and taunt him and call him names and would not stop until finally he would reveal his true identity. Unmasked, he would cover his head with his coat, leaving only his face visible, and swoop down upon the children with a terrible laugh and menacing leer, as if to attack them.

The children would run away, pretending to be afraid. In truth, they were not at all frightened, for when the witch got too close for comfort, they would turn around and beat her up. Which they had every right to do. For, as all children know, that is the only way to tame a witch! Witches are dangerous only so long as they are feared. Once they are tamed, they are fun, as the children of Broca Street learned when they tamed Monsieur Pierre.

One day, as he was sitting at a table sipping a light coffee, the children asked him to tell them a story. He complied. The next day they asked for another. Again he complied. This went on day after day. The more stories he told them, the more they wanted to hear. When his supply ran out, he went back to the tales he had read in his childhood, and thus he was able to introduce the children to Perrault, Andersen, Grimm, and some Russian, Greek, French, and Arab writers. Still the children clamored for more.

A year and a half later, having no more stories to tell, Monsieur Pierre made the children an offer: they would all meet every Thursday afternoon and make up stories together. And one day, when they had enough stories, they would publish them in a book.

This is what happened. And that is how the present collection came into being. Those who have never done creative work under such conditions cannot imagine the wide variety of ideas, the wonderfully poetic conceptions and, occasionally, the plots of astonishing boldness that children are capable of contributing.

But I am rambling on. I will stop here because it would be unforgivable if in a book of tales intended for children, a preface written for grown-ups were to occupy more pages than one of the tales.

In any case, I have nothing further to say, except to wish pleasant reading to my little friends of Broca Street, and to those elsewhere, and indeed everywhere in the world.

Tales of the Rue Broca

The Cunning Little Pig

ONCE UPON A TIME there lived a Mama God and her son, little God. One evening Mama God had settled herself in a wide armchair and was darning socks while little God, sitting at a big table, was finishing his homework.

Little God worked quietly; and when he had finished, he asked:

—Mama, may I have your permission to make a world?

Mama God looked at him:

—Have you finished your homework?

—Yes, Mama.

—Have you studied your lessons?

—Yes, Mama.

—Good. Then you may.

—Thank you, Mama.

Little God took a sheet of paper and some colored pencils and set about making the world.

In the beginning he created the heavens and the earth. But the sky was empty, as was the earth, and darkness was upon both.

So little God created two lights: the sun and the moon. And he said aloud:

—Let the sun be the gentleman and the moon be the lady.

And so it was, and a little girl was born to them whom they called little Dawn.

Little God then created the plants that grow on the earth and the algae that grow in the sea. After that he created the animals that walk on the earth, those that crawl, those that swim in the water, and those that fly in the air. Then he created man, the most intelligent of all animals.

When he had done all that, the earth was fully populated. But the sky was still empty. He therefore called out with all his might:

—Who wants to come and live in the sky?

Everyone heard him, with the exception of a greedy little pig who was so busy eating acorns that he heard nothing at all.

All those who wanted to live in the sky responded at once; among them were Aries the ram, Taurus the bull, the twins called Gemini, Cancer the crab, Leo the lion, a young girl called Virgo, Scorpio the scorpion, an archer called Sagittarius, Capricorn the goat, a water bearer called Aquarius, Pisces the fishes, two she-bears, a hunter called Orion, and several objects such as Libra the scale and lots of Greek letters.

Whereupon little God took them one after the other and nailed them to the heavenly canopy by means of heavy silver nails called stars. This process hurt them somewhat, but they were so happy to be living in the sky that they were not about to make a fuss. When it was all over, the sky was strewn with occupants and the stars were shining with the utmost brilliance.

—It's all well and good, said the sun, but when I rise I am going to roast them alive!

—That's true, said little God, I didn't think about that!

He reflected a moment, then said:

To avoid trouble, every morning before her father, the sun, rises, little Dawn will get up and unnail the occupants of the sky and every evening, after he has retired, she'll put them back into place!

Everything having thus been taken care of, Little God looked at his world with contentment.

—Do you know, said Mama God, we are getting close to your bedtime? Tomorrow is a schoolday.

—Right away, Mama, said little God.

He was about to get up from the table when he heard a loud noise. It was the little pig, running at full speed toward him, all out of breath and shouting at the top of his voice:

—Hey, what about me? Hey, what about me?

—Well, what about you? asked little God.

—Why can't I too live in the sky?

—Why didn't you ask before?

—Nobody told me I had to ask!

—What do you mean, nobody? exclaimed little God. Didn't you hear me call for volunteers?

—No, I didn't hear you.

—What on earth were you doing?

—I believe, said the little pig, blushing, that I was eating acorns . . .

—That's too bad! said little God. If you weren't such a glutton, you would have heard me, because I certainly did shout loud enough!

Hearing these words, the little pig started to whine:

—For pity's sake, little God, sir! You are not going to leave me behind like this, are you? Oh, find me a little spot! Tell the others to move closer together. If need be, nail me on top of them! But do something, I beg of you!

—It's impossible! said little God. First of all, there is no more room. You can see that for yourself. The others can't crowd any closer together. In addition, there are no more stars with which to nail you to the sky. Finally, I've got to go: Mother called me quite some time ago.

As he said this, little God got up from the table and went to bed. Ten minutes later he was fast asleep, completely oblivious of the world he had created.

Under the window, the little pig was wallowing on the ground, sobbing:

—I want to go to the sky! I want to go to the sky!

Suddenly he noticed that he was alone, and he stopped sobbing. He stretched out, laid his snout on his front paws and began to growl:

—I know quite well that they don't like me! Nobody likes me! They've all got a grudge against me! Even little God! He's prejudiced! He deliberately called out while I was eating, so I would not hear him! And he rushed through the filling up of the sky so that when I arrived it would be too late! And what does that mean —that there are no more stars for me? Couldn't he have made up other stars? Oh, but I am going to have my revenge! They are not going to get away with this! So, there are no more stars for me? We'll see about that!

He got up and, waddling along, went to look for little Dawn.

The night was nearing its end and little Dawn had just arisen. She was finishing combing her hair when the little pig entered her room:

—My poor little Dawn! he said, looking full of sorrow. How unhappy you must be!

—I, unhappy? Oh no!

—Oh yes, said the little pig, you are very unhappy! Your parents are so harsh with you!

—My parents, harsh? What do you mean?

—What? Is it not harsh to force a child of your age to arise before the day to pull nails out of the sky? And to keep her up at night just to nail them in again? The thought of it makes me sick!

—Come now, said little Dawn, you mustn't feel sick

because of such a trifle! This job of mine is fun. I am not complaining. And besides, it's not my parents' fault! It was little God's command!

—Let's not speak about little God, said the little pig bitterly.

—Oh, I am so sorry to have mentioned him if I have caused you pain . . .

—Forget it. I want you to understand that I have only one wish—to be of help to you. But if you despise me so much that you cannot accept my offer, then . . .

—But I don't despise you! protested little Dawn. What exactly do you have in mind?

—Oh, I have nothing in mind. I am simply suggesting . . .

—What are you suggesting?

The little pig lowered his voice:

—Well, if you were agreeable to it, I would accompany you this morning and help you with your work . . .

—If that would make you happy . . .

—Oh, but I am not concerned with my own happiness, said the little pig haughtily. I am here to help you! Strictly to help you!

—Okay, then. Let's go!

Little Dawn put away her comb and picked up a large bag and hung it over her shoulder, and together they left.

Once up in the sky, they began Dawn's work. The little pig held the bag open while little Dawn threw in the stars, one after the other. In this way, one by one, all of the sky's occupants were unnailed and returned to earth to spend the day there.

—This is marvelous! said little Dawn. I am going twice as fast as usual! Thank you, little pig.

—You are welcome, you are welcome, said the little pig, laughing inwardly.

And then, just as little Dawn was throwing the stars of Ursa Minor into the open bag, the little pig pounced on the most beautiful one, the pole-star, which is the star that points out where North is. He seized her in midair, gulped her down as if she were a truffle, and ran away.

—Little pig! What on earth are you doing? cried out little Dawn.

But the little pig turned a deaf ear. He returned to earth at full speed and promptly disappeared.

What could she do? Little Dawn would have liked to run after him, but she had to finish removing the stars from the sky because the horizon was already growing pale in the east. She went back to her task, and only after she completed it was she able to go after the little pig.

From daybreak until noon she scoured Asia. But nobody there had seen the little pig. From noon until four in the afternoon she scoured Africa. But the little pig had not appeared there. After four o'clock she scoured Europe.

In the meantime the little pig, aware that he was

being followed, had taken refuge in France in a city called . . . what is it called? Ah yes, Paris. In running through Paris, he had gone down a street called . . . what on earth was it called? Ah yes! Broca Street! And at No. 69 of Broca Street, he disappeared into a general store belonging to . . . oh, gosh! To whom did it belong? Ah yes, to Papa Saïd!

Papa Saïd wasn't around. Mama Saïd wasn't around either. They were both out—I no longer remember why. Besides, Nadia, the eldest daughter, had been kidnapped by the wicked witch of Mouffetard Street and her little brother Bachir had gone to rescue her. So only the youngest daughters, Malika and Rachida, were around to sell groceries and make drinks for thirsty customers.

They were having a quiet time in the early afternoon when in came a cute little pig whose tightly stretched skin gave off a soft pink light (on account of the star which was in his belly).

—Save me! Please! Do save me! he begged in a broken voice.

—From what should we save you? asked Malika.

—From a little girl! From little Dawn! She's running after me! She wants to kill me! So she can eat me!

—Well, I never! exclaimed Rachida.

—Yes, yes! She's been pursuing me since this morning! If you don't hide me, she is going to eat me!

And the little pig shed thick tears.

The two little girls looked at each other:

—Poor animal, said Malika.

—We must do something! decided Rachida.

—Suppose we hide him in the cellar? suggested Malika.

—That's a very good idea!

They brought the pig down into the cellar and were about to shut the trapdoor over him when he stopped them:

—In case they ask for me, you haven't seen me. Is that clearly understood?

—Yes, said Malika.

—Oh, I almost forgot! Little Dawn will no doubt tell you a most unlikely story about some star I am supposed to have eaten. Of course that is completely absurd: little pigs don't eat stars. I hope you won't believe her . . .

—Of course we won't! Rachida assured him.

—One more word! Don't mention me to your parents. It will be better that way. Parents, you know, are foolish; they don't understand what life is about . . .

—That's agreed! said the little girls.

And they dropped the trapdoor shut. Then they looked at each other.

—Why doesn't he want us to tell our parents about him? muttered Malika, looking distrustful. It seems suspicious to me!

—And why does he shine like that in the darkness? asked Rachida. You noticed that, didn't you, while he was talking to us in the cellar? One could have mistaken him for a lamp with a pink shade!

Malika thought a moment, made a face, then said:

—Maybe that unlikely story about a star is true after all . . . ?

—But in that case, aren't we doing wrong in hiding him? asked Rachida very uneasily.

—Too bad! said Malika. That should have occurred to us earlier. Now that we have let him in, we no longer have the right to betray him.

At about five o'clock in the afternoon little Dawn walked into the store.

—Good day, young ladies! Have you by any chance seen a little pink pig?

—Quite pink and luminous? asked Malika.

—Exactly so!

—No, we haven't seen him!

—In that case, I am sorry to have troubled you, said little Dawn. Good-bye!

And she walked out. But five minutes later she was back.

—Excuse me, young ladies. It's about the little pig. If you haven't seen him, how do you know he is luminous?

—It's because he has eaten a star, replied Rachida.

—That's precisely so. Did you see him?

—No, no!

—Oh! All right . . .

And little Dawn walked out for the second time. But as soon as she was outside, she frowned, then again returned to the shop.

—Excuse me, young ladies, it's me again. Are you really quite sure you haven't seen this little pig?

—Oh, yes! Quite sure! Absolutely sure, Malika and Rachida replied in unison, as they blushed like peonies.

Little Dawn looked at them with a very suspicious eye. But, lacking any proof, she didn't dare press them any further, and this time she left for good.

At six o'clock in the evening Papa Saïd returned with Mama. They asked the little girls:

—Did anything happen today?

—Oh yes, they said. Nadia was kidnapped by the wicked witch.

—Then what happened?

—Then Bachir went to rescue her.

—Very good! Anything else?

—No, nothing else.

—Splendid! Let's have a snack.

A few hours later darkness fell. Little Dawn had scoured the world, without success, and again it was time for her to put the occupants of the sky into their proper place. She took her bag of stars, summoned the heavenly animals and proceeded to nail them back in. When she reached the small she-bear, she fastened her as well as she could with the stars on hand and was about to move on when the small she-bear stopped her:

—Well? What about my pole-star? You are forgetting my pole-star!

—Hush! whispered little Dawn. I am afraid I have lost her. But don't tell a soul. I promise I'll find her for you again before tomorrow night . . .

But the small she-bear would not listen. She started to scream:

—Whaaa! My pole-star! Whaaa! I want my pole-star! Whaaa! The little girl has lost my pole-star!

She made such a commotion that the moon rushed over to her:

—What now? What's going on?

Little Dawn, quite ashamed, told her mother what had happened.

—Why didn't you tell me sooner? asked the moon.

—I didn't dare, Mama. I was hoping to find her all by myself . . .

—Well, that wasn't very smart. Now we are going to have to tell your father and you know what he's like when he's awakened from his sleep.

Little Dawn, sniffling away, completed her task, assisted by her mother. When they were through, they went to wake up the sun.

On that particular night, which was beautiful and clear, there was no pole-star; instead, there was a large black hole in the sky. And many ships bound for America ended up in Africa or even in Australia, because they could not tell where North was.

—Hah! That is something! raged the sun when the moon told him what had happened. What in heaven can I have done to deserve such a little fool . . . I wonder what's keeping me from . . .

—Come now, don't get mad, said the moon impatiently. What good will it do you?

—You are right, said the sun. But all the same . . .

Then, turning toward little Dawn, he asked her:

—Now then, tell me everything.

He listened to her story, then said:

—The little pig is surely at Papa Saïd's. It's clear the little girls have hidden him. Quickly, let me have my big black coat, my black hat, my black scarf, my black mask, and my black glasses; I am leaving right away.

The sun put on his big black coat, his black hat, his black scarf, his black mask, and his dark glasses. In this attire, nobody could recognize him. He lowered himself to the earth and went directly to see Papa Saïd.

When he entered the store, Papa Saïd asked him:

—And what can I do for you, sir?

—Nothing, said the sun. I would like to speak to you.

Papa Saïd, mistaking him for a traveling salesman, said:

—Come back tomorrow! Why do you fellows always come at this time? Can't you see that I am busy with customers?

—I am not who you think I am, said the sun. I am looking for the little pig who has eaten the pole-star.

—What are you talking about? There is no little pig here!

—But I am sure he is here. He was let in by your children.

Papa Saïd called his four children away from the television set.

—What is this all about? Have you kids seen a little pig?

—As for me, said Nadia, I haven't been here all day: I was kidnapped by the witch.

—I wasn't around either, said Bachir: I went to rescue her.

Malika and Rachida remained silent, their heads lowered. Papa Saïd asked them:

—Well, what about you? Have you seen a little pig?

—Little pig? asked Malika in a thin voice.

—Little pig? echoed Rachida.

Papa Saïd lost patience.

—Yes! A little pig! Not a hippopotamus, to be sure! Are you deaf?

—Did you see a little pig? Malika asked Rachida.

—Me? Oh no! replied Rachida. What about you? Did you see a little pig?

—No, I didn't either. No little pig . . .

—Really! said the sun. Are you sure? A little pig, green all over, who was being pursued by an elderly gentleman with a wooden leg?

—That's not so at all! said Malika indignantly. He was pink!

—And besides, said Rachida excitedly, it wasn't an old man who was pursuing him: it was a little girl! And she did not have a wooden leg!

They stopped talking at the same instant, looked at each other and, fully understanding that they had unwittingly betrayed themselves, blushed to the roots of their hair.

—Here is the proof, said the sun.

—What does this mean? exclaimed Papa Saïd. Hiding a little pig here! And without even letting me know! And lying about it, into the bargain!

The two little girls began to cry:

—But it isn't our fault!

—We thought we were doing the right thing!

—He pleaded so earnestly!

—He begged us!

—He told us the little girl wanted to kill him!

—To kill him so that she could eat him!

—Enough lies! cried Papa Saïd. Come here—I am going to give you a spanking!

But now the sun intervened.

Don't spank them, Mr. Saïd. I feel certain they are telling the truth. I know this little pig. He is a naughty liar and he is perfectly capable of having told them such a story!

Then, turning toward the two girls, he asked them in a kindly way:

—And where did you put him?

—In the cellar, whispered Malika.

—Would you show me your cellar? The sun asked Papa Saïd.

—The fact is, I'd rather not! said Papa Saïd. I don't like this kind of snooping around. It leads to trouble. I don't even know who you are.

—I am the sun, said the sun.

—If that is so, prove it. Take off your glasses.

—I can't, said the sun. If I took them off, the whole house would go up in flames.

—In that case, do keep them on, said Papa Saïd. And please do come with me behind the counter.

All the customers watched as Papa Saïd lifted the trapdoor, and at once all could see the soft pink light glowing from below.

—There he is! cried the sun.

He reached down with his long, long arm, lifted the little pig by the ear and put him down on the marble counter. The little pig struggled, wriggled and screamed with all his might:

—Let me go! Leave me alone! I want to stay here!

—When I'm through with you, you can stay wherever you wish, said the sun, but first I want the star.

—The star? What star? I don't know any star! I've never seen a star!

—Liar, said the sun. I can see it shining, even through your belly!

The little pig looked down at his belly, saw the light from the star, and gave up pretending:

—Well then, take it back, your star! he said. I never wanted it anyway! I did not intend to eat it!

—Don't talk so much, said the sun, and spit it up, if you can!

The little pig tried and tried to cough up the star but did not succeed.

—We will have to force it out of him, said the sun.

—I have an idea! said Papa Saïd.

He put a mixture of coffee, mustard, salt, grenadine, rum, anisette, brandy and beer into a large glass. The little pig swallowed the mixture, became quite pale and began throwing up as if he were going to empty himself of all his insides—but still the star did not come out.

At three o'clock in the morning they went to wake up a veterinarian, and the little pig was given a laxative strong enough for a horse, in the hope that it would get rid of the star at the other end. Between four and five o'clock, the little pig did all kinds of things—but still no star.

At the stroke of 5:30 A.M. the sun cried out:

—Too bad! I can't wait any longer. It's close to my rising time. Mr. Saïd, have you a knife?

Papa Saïd, who also felt that time was pressing, took out the long knife he used for cutting bananas. The sun seized it and, without any hesitation, drove it into the little pig's back, making a large gash. Then he slipped two fingers into the slit, withdrew the pole-star from it and put it into his pocket. The little pig, though he was shedding thick tears, did not make a sound: he might have been a naughty liar, but all the same he was a brave little pig.

—Thank you, Mr. Saïd, said the sun. And please accept my apologies for this sleepless night. Now I must go, for little Dawn has already begun to remove the stars from the sky. I really don't know how to repay you for your kindness . . .

—I can tell you how, said Papa Saïd. Always shine brightly. That will make people thirsty and my business will thrive.

—All right, I'll do what I can.

Then, turning toward the little pig, the sun added:

—As for you, to punish you, since you are so fond of eating shiny things, you are going to be turned into a piggybank! You will keep this slit in your back. Mr. Saïd will drop tips into it and you will be set free only when you are full of coins.

—Good! said the little pig. That won't take long!

—That's what you think! said the sun.

He uttered a magic formula in a low voice. The little pig no longer stirred: he had been changed into a piggybank.

As the customers craned their necks for a closer look, the sun slipped away. He was back in the sky in time, but too tired to exert himself, so the day was chilly and gray.

The following night, the pole-star was back at its usual place again, and the ships bound for America ended up in America.

As for the little pig, the sun was probably right. For as often as Papa Saïd drops a tip into the slit, some child takes it out, and chances are that the little pig will never be full of coins.

The Pair of Shoes

ONCE UPON A TIME there was a pair of shoes who were married to each other. The right shoe was the husband and his name was Nicholas; the left shoe was the wife and her name was Tina. They lived in a lovely cardboard box where they were rolled up together in tissue paper, blissfully happy and hoping their life there would last forever.

One fine morning, however, a salesman took them out of their box to try them on a lady. The lady got up, took a few steps in them, and, seeing that they were comfortable, said:

—I'll buy them.

—I'll wrap them up, said the salesman.

—That won't be necessary, said the lady, I'll wear them. The lady paid, and left wearing the new shoes.

And that is how it came to pass that Nicholas and Tina, for the first time in their lives, did not see each other for one whole day. Only at night, in the dark closet, did they meet again.

—Is that you, Tina?

—It is I, Nicholas.

—Oh, how wonderful! I thought you were lost!

—I thought so too. But where were you?

—I was on the right foot.

—And I, I was on the left foot.

—Now I understand. Each time you were in front, I was in back. And when you were in back, I was in front. That is the reason we could not see each other.

—Is this how life is going to be each day? asked Tina.

—I am afraid so!

—I can't bear it! To go all day without seeing you, my darling Nicholas! I'll never get used to that!

—Listen, said Nicholas, I have an idea: Since I am always on the right and you are always on the left, whenever I go forward I'll also twist in your direction, and that way we will be able to greet each other. Okay?

—Okay.

The following day, the lady wasn't able to take more than three steps without her right foot twisting to the left, and each time it happened—*splat!*—she landed on the ground.

Disturbed by this turn of events, she went to consult a physician.

—Doctor, I don't know what is the matter with me. Each time I take a step, or almost each time, my right foot turns to the left, and I fall down!

—That is very serious, said the doctor. If it continues, we shall have to cut off the right foot. Here, take this prescription: it will cost you 10,000 francs to have it filled. Give me 2,000 francs for the consultation and come back to see me tomorrow.

That evening, in the closet, Tina asked Nicholas:

—Did you hear what the doctor said?

—Yes, I heard.

—That is horrible! If they cut off her right foot, she will throw you away and we will be separated forever! We must do something!

—Yes, but what?

—Listen, I have an idea: To confuse things, tomorrow, instead of you twisting toward me, I will twist toward you when I go forward. Okay?

—Okay.

This Tina did, and all day long the left foot kept twisting to the right, and each time it happened—*splat!* —the poor lady found herself on the floor again. Greatly disturbed, she kept her appointment with the doctor.

—Doctor, things are getting worse! Now it is my left foot that trips me up.

—That is further reason for concern, said the doctor.

If it continues, we will have to cut off both feet! Here, take this prescription: it will cost you 20,000 francs to have it filled. Give me 3,000 francs for the consultation, and above all don't forget to come back to see me tomorrow.

That same evening, Nicholas asked Tina:

—Did you hear?

—I heard.

—If they cut off her feet, what will happen to us?

—I can't bear to think about it!

—I love you, Tina!

—I love you, Nicholas!

—I would never want to leave you!

—I feel the same!

Thus they spoke in the darkness, unaware that the lady herself was wandering down the corridor in her slippers because the physician's words worried her and prevented her from sleeping. As she went by the closet door, she overheard this entire conversation, and since she was very intelligent, she began to understand what had been going on.

—So that's it, she thought to herself. It's not that something has happened to my feet but that my shoes are in love with each other! How very touching!

Whereupon she threw into the garbage pail the 30,000 francs' worth of medicines she had bought and, the following day, said to her cleaning woman:

—You see this pair of shoes? Although I will never put them on again, I wish to keep them. So keep them

well polished—see that they are always shiny. And, above all, never separate one from the other!

Left to herself, the cleaning woman thought:

—Madam is crazy to keep these shoes if she doesn't intend to wear them! In a couple of weeks, when she will have forgotten them, I shall steal them!

Two weeks later, she stole them and put them on her own feet. But she found that when she had them on she couldn't walk straight and she was forever stumbling and tripping. One evening, as she was carrying the garbage down the service stairs, Nicholas twisted to the left to give Tina a kiss, and—*crash! bang! splat!*—the cleaning woman landed on her behind, her head covered with parings, and a spiraling potato peel, like a curl, hanging from her head.

—These shoes are hexed! she thought. I will never again wear them. I am going to give them to my niece, who has a problem with one of her feet.

That is precisely what she did. The niece spent almost all of her time seated in a chair, with her feet together. When by chance she did walk, she favored one foot and went so slowly that her feet simply could not trip each other up. The shoes were delighted, because now, even during the day, they spent most of their time side by side.

This state of affairs lasted quite a while. Unfortunately, the niece, favoring one foot as she did, in time used up the sole of one shoe faster than the other.

One evening, Tina said to Nicholas:

—My sole is wearing through, oh, so thin! There will soon be a hole in me!

—Don't let that happen! said Nicholas. If they throw us out, we'll again be parted.

—I know it, said Tina, but what am I to do? How awful it is, getting old!

And eight days later, her sole was worn through. The niece bought new shoes and threw Nicholas and Tina into the garbage pail.

—What's to become of us? asked Nicholas.

—I don't know, said Tina. If I could only be sure never to be parted from you!

—Come closer, said Nicholas, and put my strap together with yours. In this way, we'll never be separated.

So they did. Together they were thrown into the garbage can in front of the house, together they were taken away by the sanitation truck, and together they were dumped onto the garbage heap on the outskirts of town. There they remained, until some time later they were found one day by a little boy and a little girl.

—Oh, look at the shoes! They are arm in arm!

—That is because they are married to each other, said the little girl.

—Well, then, said the little boy, if they are married to each other, let's send them on a honeymoon!

The little boy took the shoes and nailed them, side by side, on a board. He then took the board to the water's edge and let it drift out toward the sea. As the board floated away, the little girl waved her handkerchief:

—Good-bye, shoes, and bon voyage!

And thus it came to pass that Nicholas and Tina, who were sure that life held nothing more for them, were late in life treated to an unexpected and glorious honeymoon.

The Good Little Devil

Once upon a time there was a cute little devil, with red skin, two black horns and a pair of batlike wings. His papa was a big green devil and his mama a blue she-devil. The three of them lived in a place called Hell which may be found in the center of the earth.

Hell is not at all like the world we know. In fact, it is just the opposite: What we think of as good is evil in Hell; and what is evil here is considered good down there. So it is that when a devil is wicked, he is simply behaving like a fine, upstanding devil.

Our little devil, however, wanted to be good and was therefore the despair of his family. Each evening when he returned from school, his father would say:

—What did you do today?

—I went to school.

—You little fool! You don't mean to say that you did your homework?

—Yes, papa.

—Little idiot! At least you misbehaved, I hope.

—Not really.

—Did you beat up your little schoolmates?

—No, papa.

—Did you throw spitballs?

—No, papa.

—Did you at least put thumbtacks on the teacher's chair?

—No, papa.

—Well then, what did you do?

—I wrote a composition, solved two problems, studied my history. . . .

On hearing that, papa devil would seize his horns in his two hands as if he were ready to tear them out:

—What did I ever do on Earth to deserve such a child? And to think that your mother and I have been sacrificing for years to send you to a bad school and get you a bad education so you can become a mature, wicked devil! And look at the thanks we get! Instead of yielding to temptation, you waste your time solving problems! What do you intend to make of your life?

—I would like to be good, the little devil would reply.

Each time, his mother would cry and his father

would punish him. But it did no good: the little devil was stubborn. Finally his father said:

—My boy, I have given up on you. I wanted you to make something of yourself, but I see that it is hopeless. Only this week, you were at the head of your class in French composition! I have therefore decided to take you out of school and place you in apprenticeship. You will never amount to anything more than a second-rate devil; with luck, perhaps a boiler attendant . . .

And indeed, starting the following day, the little devil no longer went to school. His father sent him to the Great Central Heatery, where he was put in charge of keeping the fire going under a big pot where some twenty people were being boiled.

But here, too, the little devil failed to do his job right. His heart went out to the poor damned souls, and whenever he could he lowered the flame so they'd be more comfortable. He chatted with them, told them funny stories—and sometimes also questioned them:

—Why are you here?

—We have killed, they would answer, or we have stolen, we have done this, or that. . . .

—Have you given any thought to God Almighty? the little devil would ask. Maybe things could be fixed for you.

—Alas, no! they would reply. Now that we are here, we are here forever!

—Not necessarily. While it's not too hot in there, give him some thought . . .

They did give him some thought. Some of them even disappeared suddenly—pop! like a soap bubble—and were no longer to be seen. God Almighty had forgiven them.

Things went on like that until the Chief Inspector of the Diabolic Boilers made his annual inspection visit. And when he reached our little devil's boiler, he blew a gasket!

—What is going on here? There should be twenty-one persons in this boiler and I count only eighteen. And the fire is almost out! What is this? So, it's no longer Hell down here; it's the Riviera, is that it? All right, you guys, blow on it and get it boiling! As for you, my little friend (he addressed our young devil), since you are incapable of tending a fire, we will put you in Coal Extraction!

The next day, the little devil was working in a coal mine. Equipped with a pick, he extracted big pieces of coal and dug shafts. This time they were pleased with him, because he was working with all his heart. Of course he knew that the coal was destined for the boilers. But his nature was such that when he undertook a job, he could not help doing it well.

One day as he was digging, his pick went through an anthracite vein, and suddenly he was flooded by light. He peered through the hole and saw a wide, brightly lit underground tunnel with a platform full of bustling people getting in and out of a little green train with a red coach. It was the subway!

LE CREUSET
ENFER SUPPLY

—Marvelous! he thought. Here I am, among human beings! They will know how to help me be good!

He stepped out of his hole and jumped on the platform. But the moment he appeared, the people began to scream and to run in all directions. As it was rush hour, there was great panic, with children being smothered and women trampled upon. In vain did the little devil shout:

—Stay where you are! Don't be afraid!

He could not even make himself heard. The crowd was shouting louder than he.

Ten minutes later, the station was deserted except for the dead and the wounded. Not knowing what to do, the devil walked straight ahead, went up a stairway, pushed open a door and found himself on the street. Waiting for him there were firemen who brutally sprayed him with a fire hose. He attempted to flee, but the police swooped down on him with sticks. He tried to fly away, but he was spotted by police helicopters. Luckily he noticed a sewer drain at the very edge of the sidewalk, and he disappeared into it. He spent that entire day moving around underground passages filled with filthy water. He returned to the surface only after midnight and began to walk in dark little streets, muttering to himself:

—I've got to find somebody to help me! How can I make them understand that I am not wicked?

As he was uttering these words, he saw an old lady

toddling along in his direction. The devil walked toward her, tugged gently at her sleeve and whispered:

—Madam . . .

The old lady turned around:

—What is it, sonny? Why aren't you in bed at this hour?

—Madam, I'd like to be good. How can I go about it?

At that moment the old lady noticed the two horns and the batlike wings. She blurted out:

—No! No! God, have mercy on me! I won't do it again, I promise!

—What won't you do again? asked the little devil.

But the lady did not answer. She had fallen in a faint.

—No luck, thought the devil. Yet she looked like such a kind lady. . . .

He moved on, and as he walked along Broca Street his eyes fell upon a well-lit shop. He made his way toward it. Through the glass door he could see Papa Saïd, who had already locked up and was preparing to go to bed. The devil knocked hesitantly on the glass door:

—Excuse me, sir . . .

—It's too late! said Papa Saïd.

—But I'd like . . .

—I tell you I am closed!

—But I don't want to buy a drink, I want to be good!

—It's too late! Come back tomorrow!

The little devil was very disheartened. He was beginning to wonder whether it would not be better for him to return to Hell and become wicked, like everyone else, when suddenly he heard a man's footsteps.

—It's my last chance, he thought.

Flapping his wings, he ran in the direction of the footsteps. A black shadow was moving toward him. It looked like a woman, yet it walked like a soldier, with long strides. In fact it was a priest dressed in his cassock, returning from a visit to a sick person. The little devil approached him:

—Excuse me, sir . . .

—I beg your pardon?

The priest did a double-take, then frantically began to make odd gestures in front of his face and to mumble in Latin.

As the devil was polite, he waited for the priest to finish, then he said:

—Excuse me, sir, I am a little devil and I would like to become good. What must I do?

The priest's eyes widened with surprise:

—You are asking me what you must do?

—Yes. What does one do, at my age, to become good?

—One obeys one's parents, said the priest without thinking.

—But I can't do that, sir. My parents would like me to be wicked!

Now the priest began to understand.

—My goodness, what a strange situation! he said. I have never heard of a case like yours before. But listen: this question is too important for a simple priest like me to decide. You must go and see the Pope in Rome.

—I'll do that, sir. Thank you, sir.

And the little devil flew off. He traveled all night and arrived the following morning. By a stroke of luck as he flew over the Vatican he saw the Pope praying alone in his garden and landed next to him.

—Excuse me, Mr. Pope . . .

The Pope turned around and looked at him angrily.

—Go away, he said. You are not the one for whom I asked.

—I know that, Mr. Pope. It is I who need you! I would like to be good. How should I go about it?

—You? Become good? Come now! You have been sent to tempt me!

—I assure you that is not so! the little devil exclaimed. Please give me some advice, sir. What risk is there for you?

—True enough, said the Pope, softening. After all, I risk nothing. Well then, sit down and tell me your story. But mind you, don't lie!

The devil did not require much encouragement and told the story of his life from the beginning. As he spoke, the Pope's suspicions melted away like snow in the sun, until the Holy Father was almost in tears.

—What a beautiful story, he whispered—almost too beautiful to be true! As this is the first time such a thing has happened, I take it to be God's will! My dear friend, I can give you only one piece of advice: I am merely a man, and can look after mankind only. You must speak directly to him.

—God Almighty himself?

—That is the best thing for you to do.

—But how do I do that?

—Very simple. You have wings. Fly as high as you can, singing the song which I am about to teach you. This song will enable you to find Heaven.

And the Pope, in a low voice, sang a very short, very simple but very, very beautiful song. Don't ask me to repeat it to you. If I knew it, obviously I would not be here.

The devil memorized the song, thanked the Pope and flew off singing the magic song to himself. And sure enough, he had hardly finished singing it for the third time when he found himself facing a white door before which stood a bearded old man. He wore a blue robe and a halo around his head and carried a set of keys. It was Saint Peter.

—You there! Where do you think you are going?

—I would like to speak to God Almighty.

—To God Almighty! Is that all you want? With those horns? And that pair of wings? Whom do you think you are kidding?

—I have been sent here by the Pope of Rome!

Saint Peter was shaken. He looked at the devil, frowning, then started to grumble:

—The Pope, the Pope. . . . In the first place, what business is it of his? At any rate, since you are here, you will take the test. Can you read and write? Can you count?

—Yes, I can!

—Come now! I am sure you never applied yourself in school!

—I beg your pardon, but I did!

—How much are two and two?

—Four.

—You are sure? How do you know?

—Well, I know . . .

—Hmm! It happens to be the correct answer! Anyway, do you wish to take the test?

—Yes, sir.

—All right, as you wish! You see the large courtyard down there? The first door on the right is little Jesus' office. He will give you the reading test.

—Thank you, sir.

The devil walked under a broad porch and found himself in the large courtyard. It looked like a school playground and was surrounded by arcades behind which one could make out large glass doors which had been painted green. On the first door to the right hung a copper plaque with the following inscription:

LITTLE JESUS
Son of God
Enter without knocking.

The devil opened the door and found himself in a classroom. Little Jesus was seated on the teacher's chair. He was a blond child and wore a shirt of coarse cloth. The halo in the back of his head was much prettier than that of Saint Peter.

—Come in, come in! he said.

—Little Jesus, said the devil, I have come to . . .

—Never mind, I know. You have come to take the reading test.

—Yes, little Jesus.

—Well, then, come here and read this.

The devil took the open book that little Jesus handed him, but when he glanced at it, he noticed that the pages were blank.

—Go on, read! said little Jesus.

The devil looked at the page, then looked at little Jesus to see if he was jesting. But he was not: he appeared to be very much in earnest.

—Well, I am listening. Can you read, yes or no?

Once more the devil looked at the book, then he said:

—But there is nothing written here: the pages are blank.

And, as he said that, the words he spoke appeared in large capitals on the page: BUT THERE IS NOTHING WRITTEN HERE: THE PAGES ARE BLANK.

—Let me see, said little Jesus.

He took the book and read in a soft, low voice:

—But there is nothing written here: the pages are blank.

Then he lifted his head and smiled sweetly at the devil.

—That's perfect.

—You mean I have passed my test? asked the devil.

—Not so fast. You did well in the reading test. Now you have to go to the classroom next door. My father, God Almighty, will give you the writing test.

—Good-bye, little Jesus, said the devil. And thank you.

—Good-bye.

The devil left and went to the second door. On it was a silver plaque with the following engraved inscription:

GOD ALMIGHTY
Open at all hours.
Enter without knocking.

The devil entered. This classroom was similar to the first, except that it was much smaller. God Almighty was seated on the teacher's chair. A handsome old man in a red coat, he had a long white beard and wore a two-tiered halo on his head. The devil went up to him:

—Sir, God Almighty . . .

—Don't tell me, I know: my son has sent you here for the writing test.

—Yes, sir.

—All right now. Be seated and write down what I say.

The little devil sat down at a desk. On it he found a pen and some paper. He lifted the pen, dipped it into the inkstand, and waited.

D
S
AD

—Ready, begin, said God Almighty.

His head bent over the paper, the devil listened closely, but he did not hear anything. After what seemed an interminable second, he looked up. God Almighty was moving his lips but making no sounds.

—Excuse me, God Almighty, sir—

—Please do not interrupt. What is the matter?

—I can't hear you.

—Is that so? Then I will start all over again.

And God again began moving his lips without saying anything aloud. As the devil remained motionless, God asked severely:

—Well then, what are you waiting for? Can't you write?

—Yes, I can, but . . .

—All right, I will repeat a third time. But if you don't write, I will have to grade you zero!

And again he went through the same pantomime.

—This time, said the little devil to himself, I am going to write down anything that comes to my mind, and he wrote:

Dear God Almighty,

I am very sad because I cannot hear a single word of what you are saying. However, since I must write something down, I am taking this opportunity to say that I love you very much and that I would like to be good in order to stay near you, even only as the least of your angels.

LITTLE RED DEVIL

—Are you finished? asked God Almighty.

—Yes, sir.

—Then hand it over.

God Almighty took the sheet of paper, read it, lifted his eyebrows, then began to laugh:

—It really is true; you do know how to write.

—Then did I pass the test?

—Easy now! The most difficult part is still ahead of you. Go to the Virgin Mary next door for the arithmetic test. Take care, because she is strict. Run along now.

—Thank you, God Almighty!

On the third door there was a gold plaque bearing the inscription:

VIRGIN MARY
MOTHER OF GOD
QUEEN OF HEAVEN
Knock before entering.

The devil knocked lightly. A woman's voice said:

—Come in.

It turned out to be a classroom again, but this one was extremely tiny, with just a desk and a teacher's chair in it. The mother of God, of course, was seated in the teacher's chair. She wore a long blue dress and a magnificent three-tiered halo. The little devil was so frightened he could not say a word.

—Sit down.

She handed him a sheet of paper, a pen and some colored pencils.

—Now, pay close attention! You have to find a three-digit number divisible by three which has blue eyes and one leg shorter than the other. I will be back in ten minutes. If by that time you have not found the number, you will have failed the test.

And she left the room.

The little devil now felt really lost. But he did not want to give up without making an effort, and he said to himself:

—In any event, I am going to look for three-digit numbers divisible by three. At least, it will be a start.

As you perhaps know, a number may be divided by three when the sum of its digits is itself divisible by three. The little devil began to write down a good many three-digit numbers, one after the other:

123, 543, 624, 525, 282, 771, 189, 222, etc.

As he stared bemusedly at the number 189, he suddenly became aware of something:

He noticed that 189 had a belly, a head and two legs. The head was the upper loop of the 8, whose lower loop was the belly. As for the two legs, they were the 1 and the 9, and they were of different lengths, because the tail of the 9 reached below the line, while the 1 did not go beyond it. The devil cut his paper in half and on the clean half drew a beautiful 189, raising the 8 a little higher than the other two digits. All that was now left for him to do was to draw two blue eyes in the upper part of the 8, which he did without delay. While he was at it, he added a little red mouth, a little nose and two ears. He had just finished when the mother of God returned:

—Well? Have you finished?

She drew close, looked at the paper and broke into laughter:

—It's very pretty!

She took the half-sheet between her thumb and index finger, gave it a little shake and plop! number *189* dropped on the desk, from which it jumped to the floor, where limping slightly it ran about merrily and finally disappeared through the door.

And this caused no one to be startled, because everything can be found in Paradise: men, animals, objects, even digits.

—You have passed the test, said the Virgin Mary. Now come with me.

And she took the little devil along. First, to the showers, to wash away any small sins which might be clinging to him. Then to the clothing store, where he exchanged his batlike wings for a beautiful pair of swanlike wings. Finally to the barber, who tried to cut off his horns. But the horns were too tough, and the barber had to be satisfied with placing over them a fresh new halo, as white as milk.

After that, they returned to the courtyard, which was very full now because it was recreation time, and the mother of God introduced the devil to the other angels.

—Here, she said, is a new companion. He deserves a lot of credit, for he comes to us from far away. Please treat him as one of your own.

There was a murmur of surprise, and an old pink angel stepped forward:

—Excuse me, Holy Virgin, but that is not possible! An angel who is red all over and has a pair of horns—why, such a thing has never been seen before!

—You are being silly, said the Virgin Mary. Granted, such a thing has never been seen before. So what? Would this be the first time that something is being seen that has never been seen before?

The other angels began to laugh, and the old pink angel admitted graciously that he had shown a lack of good judgment.

The little devil now lives in Heaven. And if Paradise were not Paradise, the other angels would be envious of him on account of his red skin and his black horns.

As for papa devil, when he learned what had happened, he shook his head:

—I would have bet on it! He acted like an idiot for so long, he had to end up going to God! Well, too bad for him! I never want to hear about him again!

If by chance you should ever go to Hell, avoid any mention of the little red devil. Down there this story is considered to set a poor example for the young.

A Potato's Love Story

Once upon a time there was a potato: an ordinary potato, the kind we see every day—except that this one was consumed by ambition. Her life's dream was to become a French-fried potato. That probably would have been her destiny had she not been stolen from the kitchen by the boy of the house.

Having carried the object of his crime back to his room, the boy took a knife out of his pocket and proceeded to carve the potato. He started by giving her two eyes, which allowed her to see. Then he carved out two ears, which allowed her to hear. Finally, he cut out a mouth, and the potato was able to speak. Holding her up to the mirror, he said:

—Look how beautiful you are!

—Good grief! replied the potato, I am not beautiful

at all! I look like a man! I was far better looking before!

—If that's the way you feel about it, said the boy, annoyed, I am through with you!

And he threw her into the garbage can.

Early the following morning the garbage can was emptied, and later in the day the potato found herself on top of a large garbage heap far out in the country.

—Pretty place this, she said, and how fashionable! There seem to be lots of interesting people here. . . . I wonder who that is over there, the one who looks like a frying-pan?

The potato was looking at an old half-cracked guitar with only two strings left.

—Good morning, madam, said the potato. It seems to me, if I may say so, that you are a person of great distinction, resembling a frying-pan as you do.

—You are very flattering, said the guitar. I don't really know what a frying-pan is, but I thank you just the same. It is indeed true that I am not just a nobody. My name is guitar. And what is yours?

—Well, I am called potato. But you may call me spud, because from now on I shall consider you my intimate friend. I had been chosen, because of my good looks, to become French fried, and this would indeed have been my fate if the young scoundrel of the house had not stolen me from the kitchen and completely disfigured me by giving me two eyes, two ears and a mouth . . .

And the potato began to weep.

—Come now, don't cry, said the guitar. You are still very good looking. Also, that experience did give you the ability to talk.

—That much is true, admitted the potato. Speech is a great comfort. Anyhow, to continue the story, when I saw what the little monster had done to me, I became furious. I snatched the knife out of his hand, cut off his nose, and fled.

—You did the right thing, said the guitar.

—I did, didn't I? said the potato. By the way, how did you happen to come here?

—Well, answered the guitar, I was for many years the best friend of a handsome young lad who loved me deeply. He would lean over me, take me in his arms, caress me, pat me, scratch my belly, and at the same time serenade me with such pretty songs . . .

The guitar sighed; then her voice became shrill as she went on:

—One day he brought home a stranger. She too was a guitar, but made out of metal, and she was heavy, vulgar, and so stupid! She beguiled my friend away from me; she bewitched him! I am sure he did not love her! When he placed his arms around her, it certainly was not to sing tender songs to her—oh no! He would start scratching her furiously . . . uttering savage shrieks; he would roll on the floor with her, so that one would have thought that they were fighting! Besides, he had no confidence in her! The best proof of that is that he kept her on a leash!

In reality the young and handsome lad had bought an electric guitar, and what our guitar had taken for a leash was the cord that connected her to the wall-plug.

—In short, she stole him from me. After several days, he had eyes only for her—he no longer so much as glanced at me. So, when I realized what was going on, I decided to leave . . .

The guitar was lying. She had not left of her own free will: her master had thrown her out. But that was something she would never admit.

In any case, the potato had really understood nothing.

—What a story! she said. How moving! I am so upset by it! I simply knew we were made to understand each other! Besides, the more I look at you, the more I realize you look just like a frying-pan!

While they were conversing, a tramp passing on the road heard them and stopped to listen to them.

—This is really something! An old guitar tells her life's story to an old potato, and the potato replies! If I handle this right, my fortune is made!

He stepped into the garbage dump, took the potato and put her into his pocket. Then he snatched the guitar and walked on to the next town.

In that town there was a large square on which a circus had been set up. The tramp went up to the manager's trailer and knocked at the door.

—Mr. Manager, sir! Mr. Manager, sir!

—Eh? What is it? Come in! What do you want?

The tramp entered.

—Mr. Manager, sir, I own a talking guitar!

—What? A guitar that talks?

—Yes, yes, Mr. Manager, sir. And a potato who answers back!

—What? What on earth are you talking about? You are drunk, my friend!

—No, no! I am not drunk! Just listen!

The tramp placed the guitar on the table. Then he took the potato out of his pocket and put it next to the guitar.

—Go ahead, now. Talk, you two!

Silence.

—Come on, talk! Do as I tell you!

Still silence. The manager's face turned red with exasperation.

—Look, smart aleck, I have no time for jokes!

—Mr. Manager, sir, I assure you they do talk, both of them. Right now they are sulking on purpose, to annoy me, but——

—Get out!

—But when they are by themselves——

—Get out, I tell you!

But, Mr. Manager, sir——

—What? Haven't you left yet? Very well, then: I am going to throw you out myself!

The manager took the tramp by the seat of his pants and *pffft!* threw him out. At that very moment, he heard a great burst of laughter behind his back. It was the potato. No longer able to restrain herself, she was saying to the guitar:

—We put one over on him, didn't we? Heh, heh, heh!

—We certainly did! And how! replied the guitar. Hahaha!

The manager turned around.

—So it is true after all! You do talk then, both of you!

Silence.

—Come on, the manager added, there's no point in being silent any longer. I have heard you.

Silence.

—What a pity! said the manager slyly, because I had a nice proposal to make to you. An artistic proposal!

—Artistic? asked the guitar.

—Do be quiet! whispered the potato.

—But I happen to be interested in art!

—Very good! said the manager. I see that you are sensible. Well, then, it's settled: you are going to work, both of you. You will become stars.

—I'd rather become French fried, objected the potato.

—French fried? You? With your talent? But that would be a crime! You can't mean that you prefer being eaten to becoming a star!

—Why eaten? Are French fried eaten then? asked the potato.

—Of course they are eaten! What did you think happened to them?

—Oh, I had no idea! said the potato. Well, then, if that's how things are, I agree. I'd rather become a star.

Eight days later, all over the town there were large yellow posters reading:

BIG WHATCHAMACALLIT CIRCUS
CLOWNS! ACROBATS!
HORSEWOMEN! AERIALISTS!
TIGERS, HORSES, ELEPHANTS, FLEAS!
AND, GREAT WORLD PREMIERE OF:
NAOMI, THE PERFORMING POTATO,
AND AGATHA, THE SELF-PLAYING GUITAR

Nobody in the country had ever before heard of a performing potato and a self-playing guitar, and a great crowd was present on opening night.

When it was their turn to enter the arena, the potato and the guitar walked in boldly as the band played a military march. To begin, the potato herself announced the number. The guitar then played a difficult solo piece. Next the potato sang, accompanied by the guitar, who in addition to playing the accompaniment also sang the second voice.

Following this, the potato pretended to sing out of tune and the guitar pretended to find fault with her. Then the potato pretended to be angry, to the audience's great delight. Finally, they pretended to make up, and they sang the last piece together.

It was an enormous success. The number was recorded for radio and television and was soon talked about all over the world. The Sultan of Petaouschnock, who saw it in the newsreel, took off that same day in his personal plane and went to see the manager of the circus.

—Good day, Mr. Manager, sir.

—Good day, Mr. Sultan, sir. What can I do for you?

—I wish to marry the potato.

—The potato? But surely you realize that she is not a person!

—Well, then, I'll buy her from you.

—But she isn't a thing either. She talks, she sings . . .

—Then I'll kidnap her!

—But you haven't the right . . .

—I have the right to do anything I like because I have lots of money.

The manager decided to change his tactics.

—You make me very unhappy, he said, weeping. I love that potato. I've become so attached to her . . .

—How well I understand you! said the Sultan, with a touch of irony. In that case, I'll buy her from you for a truckful of diamonds!

—Only one? asked the manager.

—Let's say two, then!

The manager wiped away a tear, blew his nose loudly, then added in a quivering voice:

—If you would make it three . . .

—All right, three then, and let us say no more about it!

On the following day, the Sultan set out again for his Sultanate, taking the potato away with him, and the guitar as well, because the two old friends did not want to be parted. During that week, an important Parisian weekly published a picture of the couple with this big headline:

WE LOVE EACH OTHER

In the following weeks the same publication carried other pictures with slightly different headlines. They read, successively:

WILL PARLIAMENT DARE TO PREVENT IT?

IS PARLIAMENT GOING TO BREAK THE POTATO'S HEART?

THE POTATO IN TEARS: DECLARES IT CANNOT GO ON LIKE THIS!

THE GUITAR DECLARES: I PREFER TO LEAVE!

AND STILL THEY LOVE EACH OTHER!

LOVE TRIUMPHS OVER ALL

With the last-mentioned headline were published pictures of the wedding. The following week the newspapers were concerned with other matters, and by now everybody has forgotten about the wedding.

The Story of Lustucru

One day in the classroom, the teacher asked the children:

—What was the name of the Roman general who conquered Gaul?

Little Bachir raised his finger and was given permission to speak.

—Lustucru, he answered.

This answer did not satisfy the teacher.

Later, when Monsieur Pierre heard about the incident, he asked himself:

—Suppose Bachir is right? As they say, out of the mouths of babes comes truth. Yes, I really must look into the matter!

And so Monsieur Pierre delved into the question. He

reread all the classic authors: Perrault, Galland, Grimm, Andersen, Afanassiev and others. He went out for walks, he meditated; he sat down, he lay down; he slept, he dreamed. And at the end of a week of intense thought, he was prepared to tell the story of Lustucru.

And here is that story:

Long ago, at the time of the Romans, there lived a barbarian king. When a son was born to him, a good fairy appeared and spoke these words:

—Your son is immortal—he will never die. Furthermore, he will be a great warrior, bold and brave, and will accomplish great feats. But only on one condition!

—What is that? asked the king.

—That you name him Lustucru, said the fairy.

The king hesitated. Even to a barbarian, the name of Lustucru was too ludicrous for words. However, he said to himself, a ridiculous name is a small enough price for bravery and immortality. And after some thought he replied:

—I accept.

—So be it, the fairy said, and disappeared.

Prince Lustucru developed rapidly and became a strong and brave boy. When he was twelve his father, the king, eager to further his son's education, enrolled him in a school in Rome.

The boy was as intelligent as he was courageous, and in every subject he was first in his class. Or rather, he should have been. But his Roman teachers never granted him first place because they couldn't bring themselves to say or write anything so ridiculous as: *first, Lustucru.*

So it went, and consequently, throughout his studies, poor Lustucru was an eternal second. Once out of school, he took the tests for a government job and came out with the highest marks. But there again he was plagued by his name. Though he was by far the best and most capable person for the job, he was passed up every time and his competitors were always advanced, as they say, over him.

What could he do?

Someone else in his place might have left Rome and returned home. But Lustucru was not one to give up easily. Aware that he was destined for great things, he said to himself:

—I am better than all the others, but that is not enough. To become famous, I must accomplish some extraordinary feat. But what? Let me see, let me see. . . . Here! I've got it! I shall conquer Gaul!

As you know, at that time France was called Gaul and its inhabitants were called Gauls. Well, Gaul was of course much too large for Lustucru to conquer all by himself. He would need an army for that.

One day as he was walking down the street, a beggar stopped him:

—Please, sir, have you anything to spare?

Lustucru looked at the beggar. He was poor and dirty, but handsome, young, well built, manly and headstrong.

—Tell me, can you fight?

—Oh, yes, sir!

—Do you like to travel?

—I love it!

—You are not afraid of danger?

—Oh, no!

—In that case, said Lustucru, you're hired! Raise an army for me, and let us conquer Gaul.

—Agreed, said the beggar.

—Very good! By the way, what's your name?

—Julius Caesar.

—Well, come along then, Julius, and let's have some lunch.

And that is how Julius Caesar became the lieutenant of Lustucru. Between them they recruited an army and trained it, then crossed the Alps into Gaul.

The history of the conquest you already know. The tribes of Gaul could not stop fighting among themselves. There was great discord and strife. Lustucru took advantage of the situation and soon reached the interior of the country. After that, he helped the Gauls fight off the invading Germanic tribes, which allowed him and his Roman forces to plunge even farther inland. Little by little the Gauls began to suspect that Lustucru, rather than assisting them, was actually colonizing them. They therefore decided to stop feuding and to join together to drive out the Romans.

The young king of the Arverni, a certain Vercingetorix, assumed the leadership of all the Gauls and waged war on the Romans. Logically speaking, since the Romans were only a handful of men in a hostile country, they should have been exterminated. But the Gauls, though courageous and energetic, were undisciplined and divided. And in the end, Vercingetorix, besieged in the town of Alesia, was forced to admit defeat and to surrender.

Lustucru wrote the entire history of his campaign in a book, the manuscript of which he entrusted to Julius Caesar, saying:

—Go take this book to the Romans and also bring them Vercingetorix. Tell them that Lustucru has conquered Gaul for them.

But Julius Caesar was jealous and envious. He took a reed pen, some ink and an eraser and altered the manuscript. Wherever there was *Lustucrus* he erased it and replaced it with *Caesar*. Where there was *Lustucrum*, he replaced it by *Caesarem*. And wherever there was *Lustucro* he substituted for it *Caesari* or *Caesare*. In short, wherever Lustucru's name appeared, he wrote in his own.

When he arrived in Rome, he said to the Roman senators:

—I, Julius Caesar, have just conquered Gaul. Here is the book in which I describe my achievements. And now, you will appoint me emperor.

—Oh, we will, will we! said the Romans.

—If you don't, replied Julius Caesar, I will turn my army against you!

MORE

—That's different, said the Romans.

And they appointed him emperor.

Caesar marched at the head of a magnificent parade down the streets of Rome, then had Vercingetorix strangled lest he tell the truth. He then despatched two aides to Gaul with an order to kill Lustucru. When the aides arrived, Lustucru, who had been impatient for news from Rome, invited them into his tent. No sooner had the aides set foot inside than they drew their swords and ran them through Lustucru's heart.

Although immortal, Lustucru was painfully surprised. Once again he had been robbed, this time of his rightful place in history. Bitterly disappointed, he took refuge in Germania.

The Germans accepted him as one of their own. But they were unwilling to take orders from someone named Lustucru, and they withheld from him the position of leader. Once more, our hero lost out on account of his name.

A few centuries later, the Germans invaded the Roman Empire, and one of their tribes—the Franks—occupied Gaul. You have all heard about Clovis, the king of the Franks? Well, at that time Lustucru was a warrior under Clovis.

In the year 486 A.D., after defeating the last of the Roman armies stationed in Gaul, Clovis seized the city of Soissons and ordered it plundered. All the precious objects were divided up among the officers, and Lustucru was given a magnificent vessel which came from the

Church. When King Clovis learned who had received the vessel, he went to Lustucru with this proposal:

—Give me your vessel, and I will give you something else in exchange.

But Lustucru, sick of being treated as a subordinate, flew into a rage. Raising his axe, he shattered the precious vessel.

—You already have your share. That's enough for you, he said.

Clovis left without a word. But, because he was vindictive, he did not forget. A few weeks later, when he was reviewing his troops, he came up to Lustucru, seized his weapons and flung them on the ground. As Lustucru bent to retrieve them, Clovis swung his axe and split open his head, saying:

—That's for destroying the vessel.

Clovis left thinking he had killed him. The only injury to Lustucru, however, was a headache. But the encounter made him decide to leave Clovis' army.

Following that incident, there is no trace of Lustucru for some time. Actually, it would be impossible to record so long a life in all its details, even if all the files were up to date and available.

The year 732 A.D. found the Arabs occupying the South of France. To halt their advance, Charles Martel, the mayor of the palace, led a Frankish army against the Arabs, and that is how the battle of Poitiers was started. It was bloody and lasted until evening. When night fell, each army withdrew to its own encampment without quite knowing who the victor was. But everyone was too exhausted to think about it, and soon the two camps were fast asleep.

In the entire place only Lustucru was awake. Taking care not to be seen, he left his quarters and singlehandedly attacked the Arab camp. In less than an hour he slew hundreds of them. In vain did the poor Moslems try to defend themselves with swords, spears, axes and maces. Lustucru carried on his carnage relentlessly, his own wounds closing the instant they were inflicted. When the Arabs saw this, they took him for the devil. Terrified, they broke up their camp and fled.

The following morning, when Charles Martel awoke, he noticed that the enemy had withdrawn.

—Well, isn't that odd? he said. Who could have driven them away?

—It was I! said a soldier standing at attention.

—You? And what's your name?

—My name is Lustucru!

At the sound of this name the whole Frankish army burst into laughter.

—Ridiculous! Charles Martel exclaimed. How would it sound if we said Lustucru defeated the Arabs at Poitiers? It was I who defeated them! Let that be clearly understood. And whoever says otherwise shall have his head cut off!

That is how, once again, the name of Lustucru slipped off the pages of history.

Lustucru accomplished numerous other feats. It was

Lustucru who, in 778 A.D., sounded the horn at Roncesvalles. It was he who conquered England for the Normans. It was he who drove the English out of France. Du Guesclin, that was Lustucru. The Great Ferré, that was Lustucru. Jeanne d'Arc—again, Lustucru! It was Lustucru who recognized Louis XVI at Varennes, and Lustucru who composed *La Marseillaise*. It was not Napoleon who on foot crossed the bridge at Arcola under a shower of Austrian bullets, but Lustucru. It was always Lustucru! Some even go so far as to say it was Lustucru who on 18 June 1949 stood before the microphones of Radio-London . . . But let us stop right there. To say any more would start a political argument.

We are now at the point where Lustucru is a good two thousand years old. Despite all his remarkable accomplishments, his name is still unknown in the pages of history. Poor Lustucru is thoroughly discouraged. In desperation, he goes to see the famous witch of Mouffetard Street.

—Good morning, Madam Witch.

—Good morning, sir. You certainly look sad. What seems to be troubling you?

—Well, it's this: I am tall, I am strong, I am brave and I am immortal. I have accomplished many great things. Everyone is aware of my feats, but history doesn't know that I am responsible for them. Nobody knows my name!

—Isn't that strange! And what is your name?

—My name is Lustucru.

—Lustucru? You can't be serious! Well, there's your explanation right there. My dear sir, no historian will ever record a name like Lustucru.

—Is that so?

—But of course! If you wish to become famous, there is only one thing to do.

—And that is?

—Become the subject of a song!

—But how do I do that?

—Ah! That I really can't tell you. No one can, said the witch. It is a mystery why men like good King Arthur and King Pippin, rather than William the Conqueror and Becket, became heroes of songs. What you have to do is wait. After all, there is no hurry: you are immortal!

—True enough, said Lustucru.

He thanked the witch. Then he left Paris and, resigning himself to a long wait, settled himself in a small village, where he bought a lovely house at the edge of the highway.

Months, then years, passed. All day long Lustucru would sit in a big armchair in front of an open window and watch his neighbor, a certain Madam Michel, who lived alone across the road in a house with green shutters, with only a cat for company. Studying her like that, day after day, he fell in love with her. One fine Sunday after Mass he bought a bunch of flowers, put on his black suit, his tie and gloves, then crossed the road and rang the bell. She came to the door.

—What can I do for you sir?

—Excuse me, Madam Michel, I am your neighbor from across the way . . .

—Oh, it's you! I hardly recognized you. How handsome you look! Do come in! May I offer you something?

—Thank you, Madam Michel. Here, these flowers are for you!

—How very kind you are! What beautiful flowers! Please sit down. I am going to put them in some water.

—Tell me, Madam Michel . . .

—Yes?

—Well . . . I have come to ask you to marry me.

—Marry you?

—Yes, Madam Michel.

—But I hardly know you!

—You will get to know me, Madam Michel. You see, I am tall. I am strong, I am brave, and what's more, I am immortal.

—I admit that it's an attractice offer, she said. What is your name?

—My name is Lustucru.

Madam Michel's expression suddenly changed to one of terror:

—That's not possible! You are a handsome man, there's no mistake about it. You are even quite appealing. But I don't want to be the laughing-stock of the village! Ask anything of me, but don't ask me to call myself Madam Lustucru! That is out of the question. I'd rather be single forever!

Once more poor Lustucru was a victim of his name. But this time he was in love and would not consider himself defeated.

That very evening, sitting on his porch enjoying the fresh air, he noticed a faint shadow moving on the edge of the highway.

He looked at it carefully and recognized Madam Michel's cat. He called to it:

—Here, kitty, kitty!

The cat came up to him expecting to be fondled. Lustucru seized it and locked it in a small shed at the back of his garden. Pleased with himself, he went to bed laughing and rubbing his hands together.

The next morning at the stroke of eight he was awakened by shrill cries. Madam Michel, at her window, was wailing and calling out:

—Where is my little kitten? I have lost my little kitten! Who will return my little kitten to me?

Lustucru stuck his nose out the window.

—Dear Madam Michel, is something wrong?

—Oh, Monsieur Lustucru, it's my little kitten! I have lost my kitty!

—But you have not lost it!

—What are you saying? You know where it is then?

—Well, yes, I do.

—And where is it?

—At my house.

—At your house? Oh, how lucky! I am coming right over to get it.

—Just a moment, Madam Michel! I did not say I would return it to you.

—What! Not return it to me? But you have no right to keep it! It's mine! I can't live without my little kitty!

—And I, Madam Michel, I can't live without you! Marry me and I will give your cat back to you.

—And if I refuse?

—If you refuse, I shall eat it!

—Eat it? Are you mad? I'm calling the police!

—Call the police, and I pop the cat into the oven!

Madam Michel began to weep:

—Oh, Monsieur Lustucru! Why are you so mean?

—Because I love you, Madam Michel.

Madam Michel looked at him with surprise.

—You love me that much?

—That much, Madam Michel.

Madam Michel was deeply touched.

—Poor dear! she thought. Who would have dreamed that such passionate men were still around today? Perhaps Lustucru is not such an ugly name after all. One would probably get used to it in time . . .

Then she said aloud:

—If I marry you, do I get my cat back?

—You do.

—You won't harm it in any way?

—I won't harm it in any way.

—Promise? Swear?

—I promise, I swear!

—Then I'll marry you.

—You will?

—I will.

—Promise, swear?

—I promise, I swear!

—Oh, what bliss! Thank you, Madam Michel!

Lustucru got dressed, went out into the garden and without further delay set the cat free.

Six months later the wedding took place, and as the newlyweds were coming out of the church, the village children began to sing:

It is Ma Michel who for her cat does yearn,
Who wails from her window and seeks its return.
It's Pa Lustucru
Who makes the riposte:
—Go on, Ma Michel, your cat is not lost!

—What is this song? asked Lustucru.

—It's the new song that is being sung about you, the children replied.

—I find it silly, said Ma Michel.

—But I, said Lustucru, find it marvelous.

From that time on, Pa Lustucru has been perfectly happy in his little village, with his wife and the cat. The little children, knowing how much he delights in hearing it, sing his song whenever they meet him, and then go off to buy candy with the coins he never fails to give them.

Prince Blub and the Mermaid

Once upon a time there was an old king who ruled over an island, a magnificent island set in the heart of the tropics, in the middle of the ocean.

This king had a young son by the name of Prince Henry Maria Francis Guy Peter Anthony. It was rather a long name for such a small prince, so that, as a child, whenever he was asked:

—What's your name?

He usually replied:

—Blub.

Therefore everybody called him Prince Blub.

In the tropics there is no winter. And so every morning, instead of washing at the sink, which is terribly dull, Prince Blub went to bathe in the sea. He had his

UN

own little beach, all to himself, with rocks all around, just five minutes away from the palace. And there, every day, he met with a mermaid who had been his playmate from the time he was a tiny tot.

A mermaid, as everyone knows, is a sea-borne being, half-woman and half-fish: woman above the waist, and fishtail below.

The mermaid would carry Prince Blub on her back and give him a tour around the island. Sometimes she took him to the high seas. And sometimes she dove with him to bring back shells, small fishes, crabs or coral branches. After they had gone swimming together, they would stretch out on the rocks and she would describe all the wonders of the ocean while Prince Blub dried himself in the sun.

One day, while they were talking, Prince Blub said to the mermaid:

—When I grow up, I'll marry you.

The mermaid smiled.

—When you grow up, she said, you will marry a beautiful princess; she will have two legs like everyone else and not an ugly fishtail. And you will succeed your father to the throne.

—No, said the prince, I'll marry no one but you.

—You can't be sure now, the mermaid replied. When you are fifteen, we'll talk about it again.

Prince Blub did not press the matter further. The years passed and he grew into a handsome young man. One day he came to the mermaid and said:

—Today I am fifteen.

—And so?

—Well, I still love you and I want to marry you.

This time the mermaid became pensive.

—Listen, Blub, she said, I believe you are sincere, but you don't know what you are talking about. You see, I have no legs; I therefore cannot live on the earth like a normal woman. If you married me, you would have to live with me in my father's kingdom of the sea. You would become a merman. You would exchange your two fine legs for a fishtail . . .

—Well, that's perfectly all right with me! he said.

—No, it's not perfectly all right! she went on. Such marriages are always unhappy! To begin with, in most cases men marry us for their own selfish reasons. They marry us to avoid death, because mermen are immortal . . .

—But I, said Prince Blub, I had no idea . . .

—I know, I know, but let me finish. After the marriage, they start yearning for the mortal way of life; they miss their two legs and the land of their childhood, the jumping and running, the flowers, the butterflies, the old friends left behind. . . . They are bored to death. Yet there is no escape. For they can never die . . .

—But I do love you, and I am sure I will have no regrets.

The mermaid shook her head:

—You cannot know. When you are twenty, we'll talk about it again.

This time, the prince did not want to wait any longer. That same day at lunch he said to his father, the king:

—I want you to know, papa, that I am going to marry a mermaid.

—Don't talk nonsense, said the king. You know very well that there is no such thing as a mermaid.

—I beg your pardon, said the prince, but I happen to know one. Every morning I go bathing with her.

The king said nothing further, but after he had had his coffee he went to see his court chaplain.

—Is it true that mermaids really exist? he asked.

—Alas, yes, they exist, replied the chaplain. And they are demons!

—What do you mean by demons?

—Mermaids are immortal. Because they do not die, they do not go to Heaven. Because they do not go to Heaven, they will not see God. That fact should make them sad. But on the contrary! They are madly happy! So you see, they are demons. Their very existence is an insult to the Almighty. You do understand, don't you?

—Yes, yes, the king muttered.

And he went to find his son:

—Did you tell me that you were in love with a mermaid?

—Yes, father.

—And you wish to marry her?

—Yes, father.

—Don't you know that mermaids are demons?

—That is not true! replied Prince Blub indignantly.

You have been misinformed. My mermaid is no demon. She is as sweet as can be:

—Yes, yes, said the king, perplexed.

And back he went to talk to the court chaplain:

—Hmmm! You see—I hesitated telling you before —but my son has fallen in love with a mermaid. . . .

—That is a calamity! the court chaplain exclaimed. If your son marries her, he will become a merman. Instead of legs, he will have a fishtail. And, like her, he will be immortal and never get to Heaven. As for the throne, he'll never be able to succeed you. He will live forever in the sea.

—That would be a calamity indeed! said the king in panic. What should I do?

—Tell him that mermaids are demons . . .

—I already told him that, but he won't believe me!

—In that case, you must separate them!

—That is a good idea, said the king.

And he went to see the prince for a second time.

—You did tell me, didn't you, that you loved a mermaid?

—Yes, father.

—You still want to marry her?

—Yes, father.

—You are quite sure you won't regret it?

—I will never regret it! I will live with her in the ocean and we will be perfectly happy there!

—Yes, yes. . . . Well, in that case. . . . When do you intend to see your mermaid again?

—Tomorrow morning, father, at the beach.

—Tell her that the day after tomorrow, I will come along. I would like to meet her.

The next morning, when the prince came to the edge of the water, he said to the mermaid:

—My father will consent to our marriage! He is coming to meet you tomorrow morning.

The mermaid began to laugh:

—Your father is a sly one, and all of this is a trap! But never mind: let him come. As for you, do not be afraid. Nothing can happen to me; I am immortal. If they separate us, we will meet again.

—How? asked the prince.

—Listen carefully: when you want to see me, go to a place where there is water—it does not matter how little, so long as there is a drop of it—and just sing this little song:

Find me if you can,
O mermaid my wife;
I am your merman,
And you are my life.

The next day the king, accompanied by a large retinue, went to the beach with his son. What the prince did not know was that this retinue was made up mostly of policemen, fishmongers and fishermen disguised as courtiers, and that concealed under their court attire were ropes, nets, truncheons and revolvers.

The mermaid, lying on a rock, was waiting for them. As the king approached her he lifted her hand to his lips as if to kiss it, then shouted suddenly:

—*Attack!*

At the signal, the men in his entourage rushed toward the mermaid, seized her in their nets, and tied her up firmly. And before Blub could make a move in her defense, he was himself tied up and gagged.

The king then said to his fishmongers:

—Take this monster away, cut her tail into slices and sell them in the market.

Then, turning toward Prince Blub, he added:

—As for you, my worthy son, I am sending you on the next plane to the court of my cousin, the Emperor of Russia, and he will keep you there until you come back to your senses.

That same day, Prince Blub was on a plane bound for Moscow, while the mermaid was stretched out on a zinc table in the principal fish shop of the island.

She lay there calmly, not uttering a sound, smiling broadly. Even as the fishmonger came near her with a large knife, she continued to smile. He cut off her pink tail and flung it on the slicing table behind him. When he looked at her again, he noticed to his great surprise that her tail had grown back. Moreover, instead of being white and pink as before, she had turned green all over, including her hair, and her smile had stiffened into a rather alarming grin.

Disturbed, the fishmonger cut off the second tail, the green one, and laid it down next to the pink one. This time, when he turned back to the mermaid, she was blue—from her hair right to the end of her new tail!

PO
IS

Moreover, she was no longer grinning, but grimacing in a sinister way.

Trembling with fear, the fishmonger started the operation all over again. This time, when the third tail had been cut off and placed alongside the other two, the mermaid turned fuchsia, with a fuchsia tail, fuchsia scales, fuchsia skin, fuchsia hair, a fuchsia face; and her grimace had become so hideously ugly that the poor man threw his knife away and ran to the palace to relate the strange matter to the king.

The king was very much intrigued and went to the fish shop himself to see what was going on. But when he arrived there was nothing to see: the mermaid had disappeared, and so had the pink, the green and the blue tails.

Meanwhile, Prince Blub had arrived in Moscow. He was received by the Emperor of Russia, who put him up at the Kremlin in a private apartment where trained servants could spy on him.

The prince, thinking he was alone, went into the bathroom, filled the bathtub with water and sang:

Find me if you can,
O mermaid my wife;
I am your merman
And you are my life.

Instantly the water bubbled up and the mermaid appeared.

—Hello, Prince Blub. Do you love me?

—Yes, I love you. I want to marry you.

—You'll have to wait. The test has only just begun.

With these words, she dove back and disappeared.

One of the emperor's servants had watched all of this through the keyhole. Immediately he went to report to the emperor, who instantly sent out orders that Prince Blub was never to use the bathroom again.

The next day the prince requested a basin of water in which to wash his hands. When it was brought to him, he placed it on the floor in the middle of his room, and sang:

Find me if you can,
O mermaid my wife;
I am your merman,
And you are my life.

The water bubbled up instantly, and out of it emerged the mermaid, though somewhat reduced in size, the basin being smaller than the bathtub.

—Hello, Prince Blub. Do you still love me?

—I adore you. I want to marry you.

—You will have to wait; the test is still going on.

With these words, she dove back into the bubbles and disappeared.

That afternoon, the emperor informed the prince that he would no longer be permitted to wash himself.

It was then that Blub understood that he was surrounded by spies.

On the third day he pretended to be thirsty and asked

for a glass of water. The valet brought it to him. The prince took the glass, put it on the table, and ordered the valet to remain.

Then, sitting down in front of the glass, Blub sang:

Find me if you can,
O mermaid my wife;
I am your merman,
And you are my life.

In no time at all the water began to fizz and there was the mermaid—minute, to be sure, but certainly recognizable.

—Hello, Prince Blub. Do you still love me?

—Yes, I love you. I want to marry you.

—Though the test is now over, you must wait another little while.

With these words, the mermaid dove back into the glass, where she seemed to dissolve instantly.

Prince Blub seized the glass and hurled the water at the valet's face, saying:

—Tattle tale! Now go tell on me!

We presume that's just what he did, for the next morning the emperor sent Prince Blub back to his father with the following letter:

My dear cousin,

I did as much as I could, but I find it impossible to keep your son away from water. Consequently I cannot prevent him from conjuring up that mermaid. I am sending him back to you, and may God bless you.

(signed) NIKITA I
Emperor of the Russian Union

The king read the letter to the court chaplain.

—If that's how things are, the chaplain said, there is only one solution: Transform him into a postage stamp and glue him to the driest wall in the palace! That will keep him away from water.

—That, said the king, is a very good idea. I'll send him to you at once!

He went to see his son and said:

—Would you do your father a favor, my boy?

—Certainly! said Prince Blub.

—Well, then, go find me the chaplain. I want to speak to him.

Prince Blub went to the chaplain's quarters and knocked at the door.

—Who is there?

—Blub.

—Come in!

The prince entered, and just as he opened his mouth to speak, the chaplain, gazing into his eyes, began to recite, rapidly and without missing a single syllable:

Abracadablat
You're becoming very flat.

Abracadabriny
You're becoming very tiny.

Abracadabraper
You are turning to paper.

Abracadabrall
Up you go, on the wall.

No sooner had he reached the last verse than the prince turned into a postage stamp and fluttered to the ground. The chaplain picked up the stamp and rushed with it to the king.

It was a very handsome tricolored stamp bearing the prince's likeness and the following inscription:

ROYAL MAIL, 30 CENTS

The king brought the stamp close to his face and asked:

—Do you still want to marry your mermaid?

—Yes, replied a tiny voice.

—In that case I am going to glue you to the wall and you will stay there until you change your mind.

Just as the king was about to lick the stamp, the chaplain cried:

—Stop! Don't wet it! Saliva is water!

—You are quite right, said the king, who then took a small amount of glue and, by means of a brush, affixed the stamp on the wall over his writing table.

Days, weeks, months passed. Every morning, before sitting down to work, the king would look at the stamp and ask:

—Do you still want to marry your mermaid?

—Yes, the tiny voice would reply.

That year it rained a great deal, and there were downpours and heavy storms. But the royal palace was sturdily built, and not a drop of moisture reached the wall over the king's writing table.

The year after, while it did not rain much, there was an earthquake, followed by a tidal wave. Part of the island sank and the whole coastline was flooded, but the king's palace sat high on a hill and not a drop of water reached the stamp.

One fine day in the following year the president of the republic of a neighboring island sent ten planes to bomb the royal palace. The old king, the queen and all the courtiers rushed outside and into the underground shelter. When the bombing stopped and they emerged, they found the palace in flames.

The king became panic-stricken. Blub was inside! Even though he was strict with his son, he dearly loved him. And rather than let him burn, he preferred to have him marry the mermaid.

As his men formed a line and passed buckets of water from hand to hand, the king, holding a glass of water, entered the burning palace and made his way through the flames and blinding smoke to his private office. He rushed up to the stamp on the wall and, weeping, kissed it.

He was about to fling water at the stamp when suddenly it disappeared. One of his tears had moistened it! And Prince Blub was already in the kingdom of the mermaids.

Almost at once, it started to rain, and within minutes the fire was under control. When the king's men ran into the palace they found him on the floor of his office. A few minutes later, when they revived him, they told him that the enemy fleet was approaching at full speed. The king gathered his council and ordered his warships to sea. He had little hope. Of the two fleets, the enemy's was better armed and better trained. Dejected, the king then went for a walk along the beach, the same beach where Prince Blub used to bathe as a child, and grieving for his lost son he sobbed:

—Ah, my son, my child, see what has happened to your country!

He had hardly finished the sentence when Prince Blub rose up out of a wave. While completely naked, he was not the least bit indecent, for below his waist he was a fish. At this sight, the old king began to cry so hard he could not utter a word.

—Don't cry, father, said the merman gently. You have saved my life; you have given my happiness priority over your anger. But don't worry: you won't regret it. I now am one of the princes of the sea and I will protect you. Look at the horizon!

The old king did as he was told and saw the first enemy ships bearing down at great speed.

—Heaven help us! he exclaimed.

—Look again! said Prince Blub. The ships continued to advance, but now the sea began to bubble, then to grow white, then to blacken. Little by little, it filled with strange moving creatures. One could make out here a thrashing fin, there a twisted tail, and there an open jaw. The sea was alive with monsters.

—*Attack!* whispered Prince Blub into the sea.

Immediately the onslaught of a battle to the death began. Tentacles thrust up, jaws opened, waterspouts erupted all around. The sea began to froth, to foam, to heave and churn. A thousand marine monsters flung themselves on the ships, biting, breaking open, twisting and smashing all that they could. The ships rose, listed as if about to go down, righted themselves, then floundered, nose-dived, struggling like wounded beasts, crashing against each other, some of them even thrashing about on the waves like one whose clothes are in flames. Half an hour later, the sea was deserted and calm, the horizon was blue and empty, and the enemy fleet was destroyed.

—I'd like you to meet my wife, said Prince Blub.

The mermaid, pink and white, had appeared, and the prince put his arm around her waist.

The king lowered his eyes.

—I . . . I am sorry.

—Don't apologize, said the mermaid, smiling.

—You are very kind. . . . But do tell me: are you going to have children?

—No, said Prince Blub.

—Why not?

—We are immortal, explained the mermaid. And immortal families don't have to reproduce themselves.

—That's true, the king said. But, unfortunately, such is not the case for me. . . .

There was an awkward silence.

—He is right, said Prince Blub to the mermaid. My father no longer has a successor and he fears that after his death——

—there will be disorder, the king interrupted, disorder and war. Because enemies will take advantage, as they always do.

—If that is the only problem, said the mermaid, I will take care of it. Tomorrow morning, let your Highness come and bathe on this beach with her Highness the Queen. After you enter the water, you will see a silver fish which will come to play around you. Don't be afraid of him. Within eight days you will have a little son.

And so it came to pass. The following morning, the old king and the old queen bathed at the appointed spot. A plump silver fish came and played around them, and a week later they had a little prince.

All this happened a long time ago. Today, Prince Blub is still a merman. His parents are dead, of course, but their grandchildren continue to rule over the happy island which no enemy would dare to attack.